PRAISE FOR C. S. GISCOMBE

A major figure in contemporary African American letters.

HENRY LOUIS GATES, JR.

C. S. Giscombe makes evident a genius of attention to all the determinants of any one of us, our particulars, our people. He traces with consummate art the passage of time through his own accumulating presence, his points of origin and return.

ROBERT CREELEY

C. S. Giscombe has long known that our relationships to the places in which we dwell are as much erotic as they are intellectual. And the poems in Prairie Style *are Giscombe at his best. Full of complicated desires and foxes, they invite readers to forego the fly-over, to attend to the sensuousness of the prairie at ground level.*

JULIANA SPAHR

PRAIRIE STYLE

DALKEY ARCHIVE PRESS CHAMPAIGN AND

LONDON   **C. S. GISCOMBE**   PRAIRIE STYLE

Library of Congress Cataloging-in-Publication Data

Giscombe, C. S., 1950–

Prairie style / C. S. Giscombe. — 1st ed.

p. cm.

ISBN 978-1-56478-513-8 (pbk. : acid-free paper)

I. Title.

PS3557.178P73 2008

811'.54—dc22

2008014616

www.dalkeyarchive.com

Partially funded by a grant from the Illinois Arts Council
and by the University of Illinois, Urbana-Champaign

Designed and composed by Quemadura, printed
on permanent/durable acid-free, recycled paper,
and bound in the United States of America

FOR PAUL YOUNGQUIST

CONTENTS

ACKNOWLEDGMENTS

All times are hard, which is to say that a spate of days or years is host to what come to be seen as related difficulties. I need to acknowledge the support — over the time it's taken to write *Prairie Style* — of a number of my friends. Notable among them are Steve Dillon, Julia Spicher Kasdorf, Jeffrey T. Nealon, Ed Roberson, Rick Schulz, Alice Sheppard, Sheila Squillante, and Lisa Steinman. My thanks, my love.

I'm grateful to Aldon Lynn Nielsen for his support, generosity, and encouragement.

I'm grateful to John O'Brien and Dalkey Archive for continuing to allow me to work in public.

I thank my former employer, the Pennsylvania State University, for granting me two tracts of time during which much of this book was written.

I cannot account for the sources for all the language here but I do want to name some.

I learned much of whatever I know about language (and process and working) from extended talks with my teachers at Cornell and at the State University of New York at Albany. Among these are A. R. Ammons, Don Byrd, William J. Harris, Robert Morgan, and Donald Stauffer.

"Mnemonic Geography" has its origins in Michael Anania's book, *Heat Lines*.

Enyclopedia of Indianapolis, by David G. Bodenhamer and Robert G. Barrows, was published by Indiana University Press, 1994.

I quote the singers, sometimes directly, sometimes not; among these are Harry Belafonte, Chuck Berry, Nat King Cole, Billie Holiday, Laura Nyro, Martha Reeves.

"The Black River" refers, if obliquely, to Gwendolyn Brooks' "The Last Quatrain in the Ballad of Emmett Till." She wrote, "Chaos in windy grays / through a red prairie."

I'm grateful to Forrest Gander for reminding me of Al Young's poem, "Dear Old Stockholm," the poem itself a reference to (a response to, a restatement of) the Miles Davis song, his treatment of a Swedish folk tune.

Rebecca Gaydos kindly reminded me of Kenneth Burke's definition of *metaphor* (quoted without indication or citation in "Cry Me a River"), this in her 2006 Reed College thesis on my work.

In the "Home Avenue" poem I quote Langston Hughes' 1921 essay, "The Negro Artist and the Racial Mountain." Hughes wrote, on Jean Toomer's *Cane*, that "... (excepting the work of Du Bois) *Cane* contains the finest prose written by a Negro in America. And like the singing of Robeson, it is truly racial."

I'm grateful to my students at Illinois State University for their conversation during the years I taught there. Much of *Prairie Style* has its origins in those years, in talks in those buildings.

I'm grateful to Rachel Jackson, my co-worker at the Albany (N.Y.) Medical Center Hospital, for her discourse—borrowed from in this book—on the fact of simplicity.

The "Indianapolis, Indiana" series leans heavily on Hugo Prosper Leaming's 1977 essay, "The Ben Ishmael Tribe: Fugitive Nation of the Old Northwest," in *Gone to Croatan*, edited by Ron Sakolsky and James Koehnline, Autonomedia/AK Press, 1993.

Lowpoint, Illinois (61545) is a hamlet west of Bloomington, in Woodford County.

My students at the Pennsylvania State University provided a number of sources. I'm thinking in particular of Torri Robinson (his suggestion of the title "Whatever Keeps You Out of Hell"), Elisabeth Workman (her suggestion of the half-line "something to say," from her treatise on the fact of decay), and B. Marlin Young (his telling—the first to my ears—of the "Voodoo Dick" joke, this in the minutes before a seminar in 1999 or 2000).

"A Cornet at Night" is, in part, a nod to the prose of Sinclair Ross (his story "Cornet at Night" in particular) and it acknowledges as well the work of Junior Walker (his song "What Does It Take?" in particular, with its announced saxophone interludes).

"The Black River" quotes Helen Vendler's essay on Wallace Stevens' "The Emperor of Ice Cream" that appears on the University of Illinois' "Modern American Poetry" website (http://www.english.uiuc.edu/maps/poets/s_z/stevens/emperor.htm). Vendler writes, "We cannot know what personal events prompted this 1922 poem, apparently set in Key West (so the poet Elizabeth

Bishop conjectured, who knew Key West, where Cubans worked at the machines in cigar factories, where blacks always had ice cream at funerals) . . ."

The "Camp Sites" poem quotes William Carlos Williams' "To Elsie" (from "Spring and All"). Williams wrote, "Unless it be that marriage / perhaps / with a dash of Indian blood // will throw up a girl so desolate / so hemmed round / with disease or murder // that she'll be rescued by an / agent— . . ." I was interested in the reported "conjecture that the particular pure American products Williams was writing about in this poem were an (urban) legendary band of north Jersey hill people referred to as the 'Jackson Whites,' who were rumored to have been descended from runaway slaves, deserters and camp followers from George Washington's army, and the indigenous Indians of the area . . ." (http://amnihilist.blogspot.com). Of particular interest to me has been the years-long debate about the ethnicity—the purities—of the Ramapo Mountain Indians. The name, "Jackson Whites," is considered pejorative by the group itself, a name used by others to describe them.

Writing this has kept me in conversation with two dictionaries: the "College Edition" of *Webster's New World Dictionary of the American Language* (Cleveland and New York, 1959) and Clarence Major's *Juba to Jive, a Dictionary of African-American Slang* (New York, 1994).

The drawing on the "Notes on Region" title page is by Joseph M. Guerry, the illustrator for *Webster's New World Dictionary of the American Language*. The photograph on the "Nameless" title page is from Katharine E.

Wright's *Wrong Sky* series; it's titled "Near Funk's Grove, IL, McLean County, 22 July 2007."

Some of these poems have appeared in *Berkeley Poetry Review* (edited by Rhae Lynn Barnes), *Cincinnati Review* (Don Bogen), *Court Green* (Arielle Greenberg), *Fascicle* (Ken Rumble and Tony Tost), *The Gig* (Nate Doward), *Hambone* (Nathaniel Mackey), *MiPoesias* (Evie Shockley), *Samizsat* (Robert Archambeau), *Tripwire* (David Buuck and Yedda Morrison), *The World* (Ed Friedman), and *XCP: Cross-Cultural Poetics* (Mark Nowak).

Some of these poems also appear—often in different versions—in *American Hybrid* (edited by David St. John and Cole Swensen, W. W. Norton & Co.), *Black Nature* (Camille Dungy, University of Georgia Press), *Lyric Postmodernisms* (Reginald Shepherd, Counterpath Press), *Rainbow Darkness* (Keith Tuma, Miami University Press), and *What I Say* (Aldon Lynn Nielsen and Lauri Raimi, University of Alabama Press).

The "Inland" series was published by Renee Gladman in her Leroy chapbook series.

Work on *Prairie Style* was done at two Pennsylvania locations (25 Coventry Lane in State College and 428 North Spring Street in Bellefonte) and in Scotland (at 1 Ogilvie Terrace in Edinburgh) and in Nova Scotia (at 5415 Portland Place in Halifax); *Prairie Style* was finished at 3431 Wilson Avenue, in Oakland, California.

Portions of this book were written on Amtrak.

NAMELESS

DOWNSTATE

To have the same sound, to be called by the same name.

Location's what you come to; it's the low point, it usually repeats.

To me, any value is a location to be reckoned with; I would be remiss if I didn't acknowledge how an event could be talked about like it was you or me being talked about.

Or location's the reply, the obvious statement about origin; it goes without saying that pleasure's formidable.

VERNACULAR EXAMPLES

You can always say what you are. Half the time the allegory's music,
how song goes with its cornets and saxophones. Do you have some-
thing to say to me? Closure re-gathers the shape of the original undo-
ing, the place where memory changed or picked up. Or it's human-
looking: big-boned, about as noisy, parts missing or left out, parts
overstated. A loud brother to the divine, an admonishment; I was two
men, I was something, I was "something monstrous." Jokes just drain
the spirit.

I-70 BETWEEN DAYTON AND EAST SAINT LOUIS, WESTBOUND LANES

I'd essay, I'd go toe-to-toe.

Property's a measure of elimination. Down to the left is Little Egypt, way off to the right's Prairie du Chien and the Robert Taylor Homes of recent memory.

You can work for someone, you can be lazy in the face of accident hovering in the wings.

Anyone can measure the advent of minor harmonies and melancholy. An arch at Ohio/Indiana, another—similar, more formidable—at the Mississippi. Eaton, Richmond, big Indianapolis, beautiful-sounding Terre Haute, don't forget Effingham, can't forget Effingham.

CRY ME A RIVER

Generally, value exists in relation to opportunities for exchange—seeing something in terms of something else—but for the sake of argument say that the shape of a region or of some distinct area of a city could stand in for memory and that it—the shape—is a specific value because it's apparent and public, and that way achieves an almost nameless contour.

PALAVER

Neighborhood? Proximities change on you sooner or later. There's a level of artlessness; my luck has changed more than one time. Love could be an embankment, even an esker, or Customs; or a sailing ship, noisy at the horizon. The idea was that the wind could *carry* your voice from here to there, from one side of the field to the other. I was always leaving a place at the point where I'd begun to care for it. This was the gain of singing; the devil's hungry (in a song), the devil is sweet. How do I look? Neighborhood's a little fishtail in the substances.

INLAND

INLAND IS A GROUP OF POEMS
ABOUT DOWNSTATE ILLINOIS.

(FOR K.E.W., HER BARK-SELF)

FAR

Inland suffers its foxes: full-moon fox, far-flung fox—flung him yonder! went the story—or some fox worn like a weasel round the neck. Foxes are a simple fact, widespread and local and observable—*Vulpes fulva*, the common predator, varying in actual color from red to black to rust to tawny brown, pale only in the headlights.

It's that this far inland the appearance of a fox is more reference than metaphor. Or the appearance is a demonstration. Sudden appearance, big like an impulse; or the watcher gains a gradual awareness— in the field, taking shape and, finally, familiar. The line of sight's fairly clear leaving imagination little to supply. It's a fact to remember, though, seeing the fox and where or, at night, hearing foxes (and where). The fox appearing, coming into view, as if to meet the speaker.

Push comes to shove. Mistah Fox arriving avec luggage, sans luggage.

FAVORITE HAUNT

Having lost the talent for driving and become, simply, "unavoidable," I got to be an appearance at the center of things, a common apparition, neither heaven nor hell.

No consequences, but the continent itself: this is writing from experience, this is certainty past arrival, the flat center having become my favorite haunt. I got to be an image, an appearance in the literature. (It means the same thing really, being allowed to *make* appearances and over a long time *becoming* a fixture in the imagination of someplace, famous there in a manner of speaking.)

Appearance to whom?

Staying on around the place, continental, a neighborhood man, a favorite ha'nt (or a favored one), fixed, Lincoln-esque, a little happy. Simple, but lots of folks are simple.

The open set, the open return.

TWO DIRECTIONS

To me love's an animal, not the feeling of watching one but the animal itself—blunt, active, equipped. The long body and, almost independent of that, the mobile head, the range of its movement, the obvious ambivalence. A horse in the river.

I was a sad boy in a dream on his bicycle in the marshes. Always the first question is Where? Jamaica probably along the Black River itself where the boat takes one to see the crocodiles and then there's a place to eat at the end of the tour where the tour boat turns around at a low bridge. A dream of what?

Love's an animal to me, not working one or the expectation of one's arrival, not "love's animal." Love's full of uncorrected error, the fact of it being unseen or seen and stared at, speechless beneath a bridge, eating with its mouth instead, a croc or any animal.

An island, a river, a bridge. Marshes in the dream, though bird-less; and a swaying wooden bridge and the image of a missile having gone up or come up—from where?—through it: I offered it to the boy bicycling as a kind of humorous solace for his situation, an aimless if tangential exaggeration.

(But at the end was a small train station—an archetype—, just out of town, out of the marsh, and going there I got, in the dream, to long strands of passenger cars stretching out in two directions, platforms alongside.)

DAY SONG

Nothing to the sky but its blank endless chaos—old blue skies—, nothing to it when it meets the eye. To me half a belief's better by far or one broken into halves.

Trim paragraphs of uninflected speech hung over the prairie, sound's origin. Eros came up out of its den in the embankment—came out tawny, came out swarthy, came out more "dusky" than "sienna." The sky was a glass of water. White men say cock and black men say dick. One gets even in the midwest, one gets even in the midwest, one gets even in the midwest. Eros was a common barnyard pest, now coming to be seen in suburban settings as well, a song with lyrics, clarified and "refined" both. The day lengthened like they do but everything was over by nightfall. To me, it's foxes (most days).

PRAIRIE STYLE

The direction giving out—in the business past direction then and avoiding love's blunt teeth there. Done with houses and wanting to be seen as a boundary or as a line of plot re-appearing, done with all that too. Houses cleave and, to me, it all gets hammered out in overstatement—love's a terror, a revelation cleaving to contours. Love's a terror, in town and out of town too.

I was an unqualified marker, some days the ache of an implicit region. Nothing to the bear but bad hair. Having missed the trace the first time

through I found coming a specificity hard to pronounce: river of un-
accented speech, a single voice to mark it all off. Well this is name-
lessness up here, this is inward, and nothing but the curl will do.

Love's over there, to me, the old terror.

FEVER

The spiral inward. Or, instead, the trek across as if in a wagon or on Amtrak—perpetual stretch from range to image, from splay to toe-hold, cane to cant, etc. Coming across all evil (which is not to indicate that everything has been come to but which is to suggest crossing with penchants intact and the face advertising that).

On or along the way music *occurs* in such a way as an animal could, it's an appearance that's ambiguous and rarely finite.

The point of origin, the point of fade. Fielding the question. A train trails its own noise.

Around here juxtaposition's lacking so the argument that juxtaposition might state is nonexistent. Another one's got to be made; another one's got to be interposed. I felt a restless emotional excitement from no source in particular. As though I were talking and suddenly there was the great hesitancy of the prairies.

Music appears, the voice coming not into itself but to real things such as animals. A whole slew of repeat performances coming up. Today, to me, is the opposite of relief: today's blunt-toothed and equivocal, ugly. Music does the talking, the hem of my garment just banging away on the skin.

Inland, one needs something more racial, say bigger, than mountains. Before, I'd always come, as if from nowhere, to places. Trek's out of Afrikaans but has entered, as they say, our vocabulary; I've always had a penchant for the place around speech, voice being suddenly absent in the heart of the song, for the flattest part of heat.

A TRAIN AT NIGHT

Hearing, as I will, the train cross town and the silence as well between the grade crossings except for when on especially clear nights the diesels signify themselves.

Evil's all silent. Rail around here's continuously welded. The air this far in? Dry. Linda Ronstadt singing Love is Like a Heat Wave on the oldies station. The closed set of transitions. What's your body like? What's your body in the set of places? Sometimes I stare into space, Tears all over my face. Continuous—no break—into the next section or on into a next piece. At first I'd thought being visible and silent was a context on its own, a specific-enough remoteness: known by position, known as denial. Getting even. (Evil's silent and so on but it's got its gods.)

Liken it—the noise—to love itself.

(Yet despite the specificity, how I speak of the train and it about me, all train references are fairly similar and overlap with music and engage the same restless stuff music would.)

Oh, I hear the sound of a machine working like a man, working like a gang of men: an inflection over on the west side, push crossing over shove. This is dry as a bone. Fortify me night train.

PRAIRIE STYLE

A sexual image about the prairie ought to be a good idea: it'd have no meaning in a larger context and its existence, furiously local, might make outline itself a high level of vernacular—the image might be the sum of dire and hopeless songs, more of an after-image really. Love might be, in general, a revelation but sex could have a shape or a figure with which one could remember it; the speaker could recognize it or could himself cause recognition to occur. Love might be terror—the hesitation past town—but sex could be content and outline both, until the watcher (or the listener) turns away.

Male, female. Black men say trim. An outline's sameness is, finally, a reference. Towns, at a distance, are that—how they appear at first, a dim cluster, and then from five or six miles off; how they look when you're only three miles away. Inbetween sightings is the prairie itself to get across: trek, trace, the trick of landscape. Love suffers its wishfulness—it's an allegorical value and the speaker mimes allegory with descriptions of yearning, like the prairie's a joke on us (among us). Inland's a name, a factory, something to say; the thing upon which the image verges, the thing push articulates.

VOODOO-DICK

Jokes being the metaphor for someone talking on, for voice or voices, for produced, yet endless, authority. Pity the poor jokes digging out their simple tiger pits. Pity the gap of metaphor. "Voodoo-dick, my pussy," she says—the left-alone wife says in the joke—the vernacular maintaining itself, voodoo being erotic certainty here, yawning that: a big black vibrator, easy to read, difficult—in the joke—to turn off. A joke comes tumbling out before the speech, an introduction, a formalized economy as opposed to slang and lazy talk. Lazy belief. A joke's full of speed and pauses, to mimic. A joke at the end of flawless speech—dick, pussy, voodoo. The terms represent the tale: "Voodoo-dick, my pussy."

(Voodoo-dick's the same, in structure, as the more famous crunch-bird joke: the gift-story, the same bends, the voice clanging out the end line, the showstopper. Consequence is implicit; no speakers to warm you to them in either one. Crunch-bird's the older joke, says the smart money.)

THE 1200N ROAD,
GOING EAST

To me, image is any value in the exchange. Pleasure's accidental. In any event, it's hard to measure and harder still to memorize, pleasure. Image stands in. To me, voice is that which gets stuck in the head, effected voice, or inbetween the teeth, the hiss of love. Songs, eating. Whatever love says it's no image, no consequence. This far inland, the erotic's only obvious from a distance. This far inland you need something more sexual than dichotomy.

MNEMONIC GEOGRAPHY

Inland's what I can memorize and recite, section and number, what I can manage and get right. It's pronounceable, certain that way. A quantity of heat polishes the road. The hesitation—my ambivalence —takes the place of racial variation, makes the high places straight. No misgivings, but the continent itself. If inland gives on nothing, I'm delighted; if it's empty, if I'm an accident waiting to happen, I'm delighted. It's the flat me, polished to overstatement—to overstatement's appearance—, edgeless and partial to nothing.

(TO MICHAEL ANANIA)

AFRO-PRAIRIE

Tempting for the voice to locate its noise, to speak of or from. Everybody wants to be the singer but here's the continent.

Fielding the question, Do you like good music?

Open love. In a recurring dream about the prairie, a thin hedge—along some railroad embankment—in which there's a gap to step through again and again, for me to step through, out onto the view itself. Not the literary ballad, articulated, but out onto the continent.

NATURE BOY

Air over the place partially occupied by crows going places every evening; the extent unseen from sidewalk or porch but obvious, because of the noise, even from a distance. Noise glosses—harsh, shrill, a wild card. Sundown's a place for the eye, crows alongside that. Talk's a rough ride, to me, what with the temptation to out-talk. At best long term memory's the same cranky argument—changeless, not a tête-à-tête—over distance: to me, the category *animals* excludes birds, the plain-jane ones and birds of passage, both. To me, song's even more ambiguous—chant itself, the place of connection and association. It's birdless, bereft. I'm impartial, anhedonic. I'm lucky about distance but I would be remiss if I didn't hesitate over image before going on.

SOTTO VOCE

What's missing: my country voice, the miracle singing is, to vex and hound the speaker, to outfox him. (Originally the lyrics went, "where lived a *colored* boy named Johnny B. Goode.") What's missing's the way into what's visible or obvious from a distance; or a way to distinguish that from mirage, love's floating-in-the-air door.

BALLAD VALUES

Love's a lazy slave and won't come to her name being called and called, is—finally—a poor interlocutress. The call might be a station —emanation, convergence, crossover.

The phrase—the sound—may lengthen but the variation's the same: it re-encounters the consequences again and again, it meets a standard.

OPEN RETURN

Equivocation's big enough to take the place of argument. In the literature the same animal's called by different names and the descriptions have gaps big enough to drive a truck through. One wishes for an avatar. Love's inarticulate when it does appear: it's just lazy speech — love talk — and not specific and you can't exchange it for much.

INDIANAPOLIS, INDIANA

The Tribe of Ishmael, or Ishmaelites, was a tightly-knit nomadic community of African, Native American, and "poor white" descent, estimated to number about 10,000. Fugitives from the South, they arrived in the central part of the Old Northwest at the beginning of the nineteenth century, preceding the other pioneers. After a century of fierce culture conflict with the majority society, the tribe was forcibly dispersed. Camp sites became nuclei of present-day black communities, and Ishmaelites of the diaspora participated in the rise of black nationalism, perhaps even contributing memories of African Islam to the new Black Muslim movements.

HUGO PROSPER LEAMING, *The Ben Ishmael Tribe: Fugitive Nation of the Old Northwest*

PRAIRIE STYLE

THE NEGRO IN INDIANA

Neighborhood's a joke on pleasure—they've got their shores and their white islands—or just a voice to come to like a point of no protest or no return. Voice often gets *cast* as love, rooting, love's tusk.

VACANCY

Vacancy is a story unto itself, it homes in when you kiss and are kissed. Indianapolis sits at the horizon—central, hulking, cold as Canaan. I'd be equivocal, I'd focus as much on where we'd meet or pass one another as on the lover's skill. What am I missing? I'd go on and be articulate about the ways love will dog you. Come wind. The city's a house more than it's like an animal.

ARGUMENT

"A thing that becomes terrifying to its maker"; more mayhem, poor mayhem. Or argument spoken to mean that pleasure's a fact of life. The story about the Tribe of Ishmael is a reference for you to equal. (The story having been one thing passing for multiple and that way nearly opposite the convention.) Voice "goes Company" (by its nature). The joke I was always trying to tell about Canada is that we went up there but we didn't stay. A miracle's an impulse, "an impulsive act"; a story trails its own noise. Or in so graceful a city—Indy—of open looks and stately reclamation argument is a bus between destinations, you can see it coming.

JUXTAPOSITION

Color will match anything, that's its undoing. There's one thing, then something else comes up. Saying the rhyme extends or carries an idea from place to place. Color's description; say the erotic overtakes you, like color. Sooner or later it repeats.

THE DEAR OLD NORTHWEST

Juxtaposition is a kind of melodrama. What you read to is where the place takes shape—I saw you on the horizon, I could have said, you weren't see-through. "Ohio, Indiana, Illinois, Michigan, Wisconsin, and part of Minnesota." Many Thousands Gone, said the marquee on the converted theatre.

The advantage property gives you takes the place of eros. Love would mime predicament. Some are descendants of their own property; for others history is one miracle after another.

THE STORY THUS FAR

Image stands in—a hundred eyes, the hump of the present day, wild
cards. Night's got a thousand eyes, night could disjoint hesitation, it
could equal you. Living appears and re-appears and spreads like what
you can't see. Despair *is* selfish, u-g-l-y. It was summer all over Indy—
certainty and bare heat everywhere in town, in every exchange.
Where's your gift? The big eye, "the compound eye of an insect." I'd
rule pleasure, I'd walk behind it.

(FOR AMMONS)

THE OLD NORTHWEST

The dear old Northwest, laced up at the wrist like Frankenstein, and shambling like him too, the old Northwest. (The name *applied* to that monster, in those movies themselves he was nameless and unnamed; and he never spoke, he was truly simple. What was said later, say two big girls hulking around after you, that that was the name they looked like. And you the singular passion—a blunt argument—that ranged around the dear old Northwest.)

Some questions push or shove like they were magic or like they thought they were. The monster's based on something looking enough like anybody to be a reference—you see him when you fear yourself and give him ways to talk, what he'd say if he could pick up a horn and have something to say; or make up stories and tell them in his voice because voice comes to that, voice goes to that.

NUCLEI

The parasite's having been with the host makes them equals. That is, a parasite husbands the local and measure just *falls* away: what the lazy man says goes.

THINKING PEOPLE

Leaming's essay having been a counter to his sources, among which was J. Frank Wright's "The Tribe of Ishmael" (c. 1890). Wright wrote, "There is no doubt that the family name originated from this thievish characteristic, although when the name was first taken cannot now be determined, but the family was known by the name of Ishmael when it came into Kentucky. What it was before the suffering farmers called them 'veritable sons of Ishmael,' 'Ishmaelites,' etc., no one knows." And, later, ". . . that [John Ishmael] and his mongrel hoard were so like the Indian in their habits of life, so lazy, so filthy, so primitive in their habits."

Melodrama chokes the aisle but the standees are scattered. What must the image be? A region surrounds its public. You know they see you but you're aloof, on a barge. Gear down, brothers—melodrama's indefinite but the ride has authority.

WHATEVER KEEPS YOU

OUT OF HELL

I'd sublimate; or I'd balk (over what's missing). The "basis" for color in a situation is what something adds to it, to the situation; to be specific is to have authority, a shape against the flames. What's your song, big boy? Location's where you decide what you saw.

LAZY MAN'S LOAD

For the sake of argument say a lazy man's a coherent soul or that he and pleasure share a language.

Let me end with a story. Let me end by saying I know I'll be ugly all my life. Say I'm insouciant or, for the sake of argument, say I'm servantless. Shape's the same low point.

But impulse is something else, a thing to bear up under or to recall having been carried along by; or it's a racial memory.

Five days to kill in Indy—I wandered near and very far. The most common occupation of the Ishmaelites, Leaming said, was scavenging, they haunted Indianapolis.

Let the "spare" dark-skinned men at the marges of lots on the near north side be location's finale.

Or say pleasure's elsewhere as well, say it's an authority one hears about.

Facts make a train, trunk to tail.

Indy takes the places of inland in the mind's eye. I walked for pleasure—I was the speaker crossing town to solve an equation, a voice to complete the habit. I like coherence well enough but am by nature more articulate than dependable.

I've been inclined to want juxtaposition to do its job. The devil's in the details.

Let me close in with a story, lot by vacancy.

I would be remiss. I would be remiss.

Pleasure's far.

I'm day-labor and the job's regular hell, the stretch between the mow-ing devil and the horizon or between being God and being like some animal in the near distance. The bigger the region is, the more im-portant the meaning.

Achieve and avoid, both.

One advantage eclipses the other one.

CAMP SITES

Evil day after ugly day in Indy: God's amount, intellectual property. Music might have made a difference, summer carols instead of stalking up alleys and across government lawns and, on bridges, over the White River.

One night it stormed and I stood for a while and then sat under a marquee downtown—stench of rain and also the thunder seeming to come in like flatcars from beyond the city proper.

Oscar McColloch had written that the "tendency to parasitism" is handed down in the blood to the parasite's descendents, that it's "irresistible," that "degradation" is common, not "peculiar to Indiana."

Leaming argued that James Whitcomb Riley's feral icon, "Orphant Annie," was an Ishmaelite child, "a girl so desolate."

(I'd bought a room in Jeannette Life's hostelry—the Stone Soup—on the near north side and could walk to the Archives.)

BIG TOWNS

If you put a monster in a big town there'll be a story you can open like
a book but you need the town, the monster being just old terror with-
out it—a roaming hull, a speech balloon. You need a grid (for temp-
tation to have come to location). I'd be the same whether I tried to get
closer to love or not; I'd dawdle or I'd inch in, either way. Let love rub
itself up against pleasure. You need some boulevards for the monster
to cross like he was anybody coming through the camp.

LIGHT, BRIGHT, ETC.

Or skin's the inevitable appearance, the only castle (location only equaling voice). Skin meets the weave and you're clean; inland's no delta.

Skin's blank, though, and you can see it coming or going from far away. Neck to neck, side by side, a panoply of advantageous positions. Skin stands in; whole stories have to do with being caught up with on the road. Half-certain's different.

For the sake of argument, let image be the writhing end of hoop-la. I'm as interested as I should be. Let tomorrow come.

NEGROMANIA, NEGROPHILIA, NEGROPHOBIA

Indianapolis on the q.t.: camp sites, no consequences. My heart's empty, houses are empty too. Music streaming by like it was the fever of life. Neither paradise nor hell but here you appear; shape's just patter to me.

Indy sub rosa. Between us—one articulate skin to the next—location is where you stop reading.

Miraculous Indianapolis. I wanted neither faith nor affection; I wanted a telephone voice and a voice I would sin in. I'd be invisible if I wasn't so lazy. I'd be you and something else. A shape's got no door.

BALLAD VALUES

I like "short grass" and the way we sang once—James Hamilton and I sang once—about liking meat that's close to the bone. And I prefer going over the junctions to being part of the argument. I like two buses rocking perilously close and metaphor judging you. I'm partial to ugly. I vary about the point where pleasure's a train of waves. I see how voice is a joke on passion and value the smooth as well as the sweet report. I like it once you get past the natural boundary.

REPUBLICAN NATIONAL
CONVENTION, 2000

Fearsome old camp songs on television! Erotic certainty might be a
way to the border. (A white actor playing me, shouting; but for now
what's the word between us, brother?)

The convention makes much of wild cards, love's face turning up like
evil at the window, like evil looking in. On cable: naked black girls in
ancient Rome, naked as the white girls in the same movie though not
as numerous. If skin's inevitable so is ash. The convention is seam-
less — tones passing for a zenith of human understanding — but it's just
faces to me, the viewer in Indianapolis.

You can carry pleasure too, prosaic or opaque as that may have to be.

1304 NORTH CENTRAL AVENUE

INDIANAPOLIS, INDIANA

To me, intention's a fact, a register equal to any other value. Intention's the *device* in nature. It repeats the range. I like that it's noisy or can be; I like that it's a measure. The median is full of images. Argument's there to discern, to straighten you out. To me, meaning's like parallel streets. Meaning stands in. Nothing's more sexual than laziness. I'd be equivocal, I'd pass.

PRAIRIE STYLE

*I use the word "Negro" in the sense in which it is
commonly used in the United States, to designate a
person with any discernible amount of Negro blood.*

EMMA LOU THORNBROUGH
The Negro in Indiana (1957)

Situation's the uncertain argument; the neighborhood can't contain
it though it starts because of the neighborhood. The contour property
gives you takes the place of region.

A CORNET AT NIGHT

I'm the fish horn, I'm going to lean out and blow for you.

Say I'm a fact of nature, a habit of life, the broad ripple. Say I'm a Usonian. Say I'm from out past the turnaround but have come in like a pack of dogs to reveal eros to you, to converse with you about the repeating shape. Say I'm teeth and crows. Say I'm voodoo-dick. Say I cleave to you or say I'm a vacant seat pulling away from the curb. Say I'm incomplete without you, sugar. Say I'm late but say how I'll come sooner or later. Say I'm doubtless. Say I'm lazy but articulate.

NOTES ON REGION

-corn (kôrn), [< L. *cornu*, a horn], a terminal combining form meaning *horn*, as in *Capricorn, unicorn*.
Corn., 1. Cornish. 2. Cornwall.
cor·na·ceous (kôr-nā'shəs), *adj.* [< Mod. L. *Cornaceae*, name of the order < *cornus;* see CORNEL], of a large group of shrubs and herbs of the dogwood family.
Corn Belt, the region in the Middle West where much corn is raised: it extends from central Ohio to central Kansas and Nebraska.
corn borer, a moth larva that feeds on corn, etc.
corn bread, bread made of corn meal.
corn·cake (kôrn'kāk'), *n.* johnnycake.
corn·cob (kôrn'kob'), *n.* 1. the woody core of an ear of corn, on which the kernels grow in rows. 2. a corncob pipe.
corncob pipe, a tobacco pipe with a bowl made of a hollowed piece of dried corncob.
corn cockle, a tall weed of the pink family, with flat, purple-red flowers, which often grows in grainfields.
corn color, light yellow.
corn crake, a brown, short-billed European bird of the rail family, often found in grainfields.
corn·crib (kôrn'krib'), *n.* a small, ventilated structure for storing corn.
corn·dodg·er (kôrn'doj'ēr), *n.* 1. a bread made of corn meal baked or fried hard in small pones. 2. such a pone. Also **corn-dodger, corn dodger**.

cor·ner·wise (kôr'nēr-wīz'), *adv.* [*corner* + -*wise*], 1. with the corner to the front; so as to form a corner. 2. from one corner to an opposite corner; diagonally.
cor·net (kôr-net' *for 1;* kôr'nit, kôr-net' *for 2, 3, 4*), *n.* [ME.; OFr., dim. of *corn*, a horn < L. *cornu*, a horn], 1. a brass-wind musical instrument of the trumpet class, having three valves worked by pistons: abbreviated **cor.** 2. a piece of paper twisted like a cone, for holding sugar, candy, etc. 3. the spreading, white headdress that a Sister of Charity wears. 4. formerly, a British cavalry officer of the lowest rank, who carried his troop's flag.

CORNET

cor·net-à-pis·tons (kôr'nit-ə-pis'tənz; Fr. kôr'ne'à'-pēs'tôn'), *n.* [*pl.* CORNETS-À-PISTONS (kôr'nets-; Fr. kôr'ne'zà'pēs'tôn')], a cornet (musical instrument).
cor·net·cy (kôr'nit-si), *n.* [*pl.* CORNETCIES (-siz)], [Obs.], the rank or commission of a cornet (cavalry officer).
cor·net·tist, cor·net·ist (kôr-net'ist), *n.* a cornet player.
corn·fed (kôrn'fed'), *adj.* 1. fed on corn. 2. [Slang], countrified; healthy and strong but unsophisticated.
corn·field (kôrn'fēld'), *n.* a field in which corn is grown.

PRAIRIE STYLE

After dark you can always see lights in the distance, no matter how far between towns you get—lights "punctuate" Illinois. Pleasure has its locales and gateways but tomorrow's just inevitable, tomorrow's the same as today.

Argument equals your predicament. To me, it—argument—is nothing less than personal. It's like singing or lying. Your voice carries in an argument.

THREE DREAMS

1.

I was dreaming of Dayton, Ohio, my grade school, etc. Behind the school the playground extended only up to the road that went to the Sherwood Twin's drive-in's north screen and we were playing there — on the grass — at night, full moon on us. Our clothes were on but all of us in short sleeves and short pants, summer clothes. On the road your race changed, you'd be black or white depending on what you were on the grass playground, if you trod on the road. "If you go on the road," we said, laughing. Play going on, the game coming to the punchline again and again, to get or have the other race on the gravel road to the screen. Laughing behind our hands, covering our faces, this behind Jane Addams School in Dayton. The change felt like magic, we said, it went right through you.

2.

That I was architect of a regional plan, a transportation authority, a system of large and small buses and light rail vehicles. But that at the celebration in my honor I was deaf, alone, or maybe dead or nearly dead on the far side of a hill where it—the hill—sloped down to some water, to a wide river or lake. There and in the ballroom at once. (My idea had been that the erotic might best and most effectively be glimpsed in passing, named by the fact of transit; transit does that in part—

where the placard says the bus will go, you go. You can predict, but only in part, how the *trip* will go—a train or bus arriving at pre-arranged points, the schematic diagram itself, and then the "complication" of an open return.)

3.

Invited (in the dream) to a party, the theme of which was "Sex and Sexual After-images," to take place at a house on Route 11, south of Syracuse, N.Y. (In town U.S. 11's Salina Street but it starts at New York's border with Quebec and I've driven on it as well in sub-industrial Birmingham—surprised to come across it there but why not?—in the new south.)

But in the dream it was ahead, that we were going to step out onto the porch, tease one another with our mouths and then lean against the wood railing in full view of neighbors and whatever traffic. Inside we were eating, our clothes off already or half-off. En-masse at a long table, arms poised, eating food off red plates and more was coming. *Look ahead* had been the slogan. Upstate, downstate. We were mixed, we were in no hurry.

HOME AVENUE

Cincinnati's the border town but Dayton is "like the singing of Robeson." The West Side, really the city's southwest quarter or so, is black Dayton—south of Wolf Creek, west of the Miami River—though nowadays black people live all over town except of course in Oakwood. Or singing's a memory.

Neighborhood to neighborhood to neighborhood, Home Avenue is a street winding across the West Side to enter the V. A. hospital and residence, the Soldiers' Home. The West Side's no island but it has its watercourses: there's a floodplain and then the ground rises, this is the west side of the Miami River's valley. The railroad—that used to go to Indianapolis and St. Louis—follows Wolf Creek on out of town. Home Avenue's barely allegorical; memory tops it. Memory's ever-changing, it's the more peevish side of impulse.

CANADIAN NIGHTS

You said, "the transition *is* happiness." I'd wanted to drive out to the end of the continent and I have. Erotic certainty might be the way to a *city* at the border—an irreversible value, the shape of essay and desolation. How complete does the transition need to be? The joke I was always trying to tell wasn't really about Canada but about the "extent of overlapping." It's been mackerel skies all day. As you know, I'm still a nature boy. Looking back I wanted—I want—to equal the whole prairie.

(BARRY MCKINNON, "IN THE MILLENNIUM/60")

VERY FAR

Coming back on 150 from the movies in Urbana and there a healthy
fox was in the high-beams, a trick for the eyes—how the snout and ears
bobbed upward for a moment, his big head thrown back. Pale—it goes
without saying—but fast.

What doesn't change? What's the central disappointment? That it—
the long evening—was a single place? (But I always see animals when
I travel, birds too. Dusk to dawn, Mistah Fox is out on night patrol.
There's little surprising about a location; I'd say Mistah Fox can match
or resist the prairie with equal success.)

(FOR M.)

THE BLACK RIVER

On the popular Black River tours crocodiles approach the boat when
the captain calls them. Paradise is full of tremendous images. Love
having been a slave here, the serving implicit in love-talk. (Black
River's a town too at the river's mouth where it—the river—meets the
Caribbean, the deep blue sea, the water *around* little Jamaica.) Love
in the commonest sense, love in the sense of relief.

Jamaica's economic success over the years has to do with it being palat-
able to Europeans and Americans. But we were in with black tourists
from Great Britain, three young couples. Other boats from compet-

ing charters would pass—we met two as we went upstream from town —chockablock with white people. The crocodiles made a small commotion in the river—the glide forward for pieces of chicken (held out, on a stick, by the captain), a long grim face and chops in limpid water.

The island's railroad carries bauxite, the raw aluminum; the overnight passenger service from Kingston to Mo' Bay is a thing of the past, a memory. At the north coast resorts whites are or can be nude all day. Black River's southern Jamaica, Black River Port having been where the famous "cargo" ship—the *Zorg* or *Zong*—finally landed. The Giscombes are from Portland Parish, and Belcarres, but have spread, notably to Britain, America, and Canada. You know how we are. The Black River tours stop at a low bridge where a woman sells crab rolls, shrimp rolls, and cans of soda out of a small house—or this is how it went, how the tour paused the time when we were in Jamaica; we snacked and returned but the river's navigable, say the internet sites, past that, "beyond the morass," they say (mentioning the low bridge).

The region itself? Like anyplace, it's got its big towns—Kingston but also Havana and Caracas and "American" locations to the north as well, New Orleans, say, and Key West where, whites recalled, "Cubans worked at the machines in cigar factories, where blacks always had ice cream at funerals . . ."

The river's called the Black River because although its water is clear the peat moss bottom—in the morass—is very dark, this being a thing of overwhelming visual moment. It rises in the Santa Cruz Mountains, in the Cockpit Country, and is shallow where we were though it has got some deep holes; shrimp fishermen had stood up in water up to their swim-trunks as the tour boat passed—young and very dark, solid, with cheap light-colored goggles around their necks, with no hair visible on their chests. We were living downstate then and had driven north to Chicago and tumbled out the Eisenhower to O'Hare and flown in from that—from Chicago, from the "red prairie" of which Chicago's an emblem—changing to the Kingston plane in Miami.

"This is his house, I'll see if he's home," the captain would say. And then would shout the name of the crocodile.

PRAIRIE STYLE

The prairie appeared suddenly, like it was a miracle or a fortification. Trace to predicament. The trees gave way—no surprise but it was further than we'd imagined. Servantless, shoreless, nothing to it when it met the horizon.

SELECTED DALKEY ARCHIVE PAPERBACKS

Etienne Gilson, *The Arts of the Beautiful* ▪
   Forms and Substances in the Arts
C. S. Giscombe, *Giscome Road* ▪ *Here*
Douglas Glover, *Bad News of the Heart* ▪
   The Enamoured Knight
Witold Gombrowicz, *A Kind of Testament*
Karen Elizabeth Gordon, *The Red Shoes*
Georgi Gospodinov, *Natural Novel*
Juan Goytisolo, *Count JulianMakbara* ▪ *Marks of Identity*
Patrick Grainville, *The Cave of Heaven*
Henry Green, *Blindness* ▪ *Concluding* ▪ *Doting* ▪ *Nothing*
Jiří Gruša, *The Questionnaire*
Gabriel Gudding, *Rhode Island Notebook*
John Hawkes, *Whistlejacket*
Aidan Higgins, *A Bestiary* ▪ *Bornholm Night-Ferry* ▪
   Flotsam and Jetsam ▪ *Langrishe, Go Down* ▪
   Scenes from a Receding Past ▪ *Windy Arbours*
Aldous Huxley, *Antic Hay* ▪ *Crome Yellow* ▪ *Point Counter
   Point* ▪ *Those Barren Leaves* ▪ *Time Must Have a Stop*
Mikhail Iossel and Jeff Parker, eds., *Amerika:
   Contemporary Russians View the United States*
Gert Jonke, *Geometric Regional Novel* ▪
   Homage to Czerny
Jacques Jouet, *Mountain R*
Hugh Kenner, *The Counterfeiters* ▪ *Flaubert, Joyce and
   Beckett: The Stoic Comedians* ▪ *Joyce's Voices*
Danilo Kiš, *Garden, Ashes* ▪ *A Tomb for Boris Davidovich*
Aiko Kitahara, *The Budding Tree: Six Stories of Love in
   Edo*
Anita Konkka, *A Fool's Paradise*
George Konrád, *The City Builder*
Tadeusz Konwicki, *A Minor Apocalypse* ▪
   The Polish Complex
Menis Koumandareas, *Koula*
Elaine Kraf, *The Princess of 72nd Street*
Jim Krusoe, *Iceland*
Ewa Kuryluk, *Century 21*
Eric Laurrent, *Do Not Touch*
Violette Leduc, *La Bâtarde*
Deborah Levy, *Billy and Girl* ▪ *Pillow Talk
   in Europe and Other Places*
José Lezama Lima, *Paradiso*
Rosa Liksom, *Dark Paradise*
Osman Lins, *Avalovara* ▪ *The Queen of the
   Prisons of Greece*

Alf Mac Lochlainn, *The Corpus in the Library* ▪
   Out of Focus
Ron Loewinsohn, *Magnetic Field(s)*
Brian Lynch, *The Winner of Sorrow*
D. Keith Mano, *Take Five*
Micheline Aharonian Marcom, *The Mirror in the Well*
Ben Marcus, *The Age of Wire and String*
Wallace Markfield, *Teitlebaum's Window* ▪
   To an Early Grave
David Markson, *Reader's Block* ▪ *Springer's Progress* ▪
   Wittgenstein's Mistress
Carole Maso, *AVA*
Ladislav Matejka and Krystyna Pomorska, eds., *Readings
   in Russian Poetics: Formalist and Structuralist Views*
Harry Mathews, *The Case of the Persevering Maltese:
   Collected Essays* ▪ *Cigarettes* ▪ *The Conversions* ▪ *The
   Human Country: New and Collected Stories* ▪ *The Jour-
   nalist* ▪ *My Life in CIA* ▪ *Singular Pleasures* ▪ *The Sink-
   ing of the Odradek Stadium* ▪ *Tlooth* ▪ *20 Lines a Day*
Robert L. McLaughlin, ed, *Innovations: An Anthology
   of Modern & Contemporary Fiction*
Herman Melville, *The Confidence-Man*
Amanda Michalopoulou, *I'd Like*
Steven Millhauser, *The Barnum Museum* ▪ *In the Penny
   Arcade*
Ralph J. Mills, Jr., *Essays on Poetry*
Olive Moore, *Spleen*
Nicholas Mosley, *Accident* ▪ *Assassins* ▪ *Catastrophe Prac-
   tice* ▪ *Children of Darkness and Light* ▪ *Experience and
   Religion* ▪ *The Hesperides Tree* ▪ *Hopeful Monsters* ▪
   Imago Bird ▪ *Impossible Object* ▪ *Inventing God* ▪ *Judith*
   ▪ *Look at the Dark* ▪ *Natalie Natalia* ▪ *Serpent* ▪ *Time at
   War* ▪ *The Uses of Slime Mould: Essays of Four Decades*
Warren F. Motte, Jr., *Fables of the Novel: French Fiction
   since 1990* ▪ *Fiction Now: The French Novel in the 21st
   Century* ▪ *Oulipo: A Primer of Potential Literature*
Yves Navarre, *Our Share of Time* ▪ *Sweet Tooth*
Dorothy Nelson, *In Night's City* ▪ *Tar and Feathers*
Wilfrido D. Nolledo, *But for the Lovers*
Flann O'Brien, *At Swim-Two-Birds* ▪ *At War* ▪ *The Best of
   Myles* ▪ *The Dalkey Archive* ▪ *Further Cuttings* ▪ *The
   Hard Life* ▪ *The Poor Mouth* ▪ *The Third Policeman*
Claude Ollier, *The Mise-en-Scène*
Patrik Ouředník, *Europeana*
Fernando del Paso, *Palinuro of Mexico*

SELECTED DALKEY ARCHIVE PAPERBACKS

FOR A FULL LIST OF PUBLICATIONS, VISIT: WWW.DALKEYARCHIVE.COM